Building Sandcastles

Kieran is at the sandpit with his dad. He is building a sandcastle.

It Won't Work!

By Janine Amos and Annabel Spenceley
Consultant Rachael Underwood

CHERRYTREE BOOKS

A CHERRYTREE BOOK

This edition first published in 2007
by Cherrytree Books, part of
The Evans Publishing Group
2A Portman Mansions
Chiltern Street
London
W1U 6NR

© Evans Brothers Limited 2007

Printed in China

British Library Cataloguing in Publication Data.
Amos, Janine
  It won't work!. - (Good friends)
  1. Frustration - Pictorial works - Juvenile fiction
  2. Children's stories - Pictorial works
  I. Title II. Spenceley, Annabel III. Underwood, Rachael
  823.9'14[J]

ISBN 1842344188
13 digit ISBN 978 184234 4187

CREDITS
Editor: Louise John
Designer: D.R.ink
Photography: Gareth Boden
Production: Jenny Mulvanny
Based on the original edition of It Won't Work! published in 1999

With thanks to our models:
Building Sandcastles
Kieran Cox-Henry and Mark Cox
The Marble Game
Genevieve Miles

VISIT OUR WEBSITE
www.evansbooks.co.uk

Kieran fills his bucket with sand. He pats it down hard.

He turns the bucket over...
and the sand falls straight out.

"Agh!" shouts Kieran.
"It won't work!"

Kieran stamps his feet
and bursts into tears.

Dad puts down his paper. "You sound very angry, Kieran," he says.

Kieran cries even louder.

"I can't do it!" he shouts.

How does Kieran feel?

"Is it difficult building with this sand?" asks Dad.

"Yes," says Kieran. "It just falls out of the bucket."

"What could you do to make it work better?" asks Dad. Kieran thinks.

He watches his dad have a drink of water. "I know, I'll make the sand wet!" he says.

Kieran mixes water into the dry sand.

"Will it work now?" he wonders.

"I've done it!" smiles Kieran.

How does Kieran feel now?

The Marble Game

Genevieve is building her new marble run.

She puts on the last piece. Now she is ready to send down a marble.

Plop! The marble falls straight through.

"It won't work!"
thinks Genevieve.

**How does
Genevieve feel?**

"What can I do?" she wonders. She has a look at the picture on the box.

She checks all
the pieces.

"Yes!" says Genevieve, "here's the problem!"

She turns the big
green piece around.

Genevieve tests
the game again.

This time the marble rolls all the way along the run and knocks the dominoes down!

TEACHER'S NOTES

By reading these books with young children and inviting them to answer the questions posed in the tex
the children can actively work towards aspects of the PSHE and Citizenship curriculum.

Develop confidence and responsibility and making the most of their abilities by
• recognising what they like and dislike, what is fair and unfair and what is right and wrong
• to share their opinions on things that matter to them and explain their views
• to recognise, name and deal with their feelings in a positive way

Develop good relationships and respecting the differences between people
• to recognise how their behaviour affects others
• to listen to other people and play and work co-operatively
• to identify and respect the difference and similarities between people

By using some simple follow up and extension activities, children can also work towards

Citizenship KS1
• to recognise choices that they can make and recognise the difference between right and wrong
• to realise that people and living things have needs, and that they have a responsibility to meet them
• that family and friends should care for each other

EXTENSION ACTIVITY
Drama
• Read through the two stories in *It Won't Work!* Ask the children the questions posed in the text on
  pages 11, 18 and 24.
• Ask the children to remember and retell the stories out loud. Ask them if they can think of situations
  where they have been frustrated by something not going to plan or something not working. If
  appropriate list some of the ideas on a whiteboard.
• Put the children into groups of 3 ensuring a good mixture of confidence and group work skill. Ask the
  children to make up a small 'play' about a situation where something they are trying to do doesn't
  work. The play should finish at the point where the child says 'It won't work!'. You may wish to set
  some boundaries such as no touching or nasty words.
• Give them 3-5 minutes to devise and practise their play.
• When they have acted out their play in front of the class, invite volunteers from the 'audience' to
  suggest solutions. Ask 'What could he/she do to make it work?' or 'How could the problem be solved?
• Sit the children in a circle and talk about the different feelings you might have when things don't
  work properly. Discuss how it is better to be calm and think things through carefully, instead of losir
  your temper.

These activities can be repeated on subsequent days using the other story in the book or with other
stories in the series.